Marvellous Manners

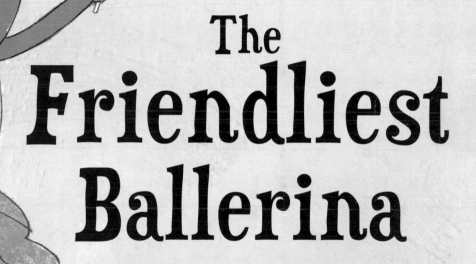

The Friendliest Ballerina

Timothy Knapman

Illustrated by **Jimothy Oliver**

D0308522

QED Publishing

Bella **loves** her ballet class –
she's the **best** dancer by far.

Today they've got a show to prepare,
and **Bella** will be the star.

But then Miss comes to Bella and says,
"This is Peter and Clare, **they're new.**

Bella, would you **take care** of them
and show them what they should do?"

Peter is small and Clare is shy,
so Bella says, "Welcome! Hello!

"I'm **so glad** you've joined us – it's just the right time.
You'll both get to be in **our show!**"

Bella **shows** them where to hang up their coats,
she **tells** them what everything's for.

She **helps** them **make friends** with everyone else,
she couldn't do anything more!

But **not long ago**, if you'd asked for her **help**,
Bella would have said, "Sorry, **but no!**"

"I'm **far too busy** to **help** anyone - you see, I am the **star** of the **show!**"

Back then she danced in the **spotlight,**
where she shone like a star - **on her own.**

But **after** the show, when the lights had gone out,
Bella felt **sad** and **alone**.

"Of course!" Bella thought. "What a **silly** I've been! Being **happy** or **sad** all depends, not on being the star of the show, but on whether you've got any **friends!**"

So **now** look at Bella - how **happy** she is,
as she dances with Peter and Clare!

Peter is small, but he jumps very **high**,
while Clare **spins** and **twirls** everywhere.

Then in no time, it seems, it's the **night** of the **show** -
Bella's **nervously** waiting to start.

Then Clare comes along and gives Bella a **hug** and a "**thank you**" that warms Bella's heart.

Bella **springs** out on stage and she dances so well
that the Mummies and Daddies all **cheer**.

Bella's never been better and we know why –
it's because her **two friends are near**.

It's good to be the star of the show,
but **remember** how our story ends.

It's sad to be **lonely** so never forget,
to **smile**, **help out** and **make friends**.

Next steps

★ After reading the story, have another look at the front cover of the book together. Ask your child to describe the picture of the girl. Discuss what she is doing and what she is wearing.

★ Ask your child whether they like to dance. At this point, it would be good to talk about ballet and describe the picture on the first page.

★ Talk about why Bella enjoyed her dance class.

★ Bella used to feel sad and lonely. Ask your child what made her feel that way. Then discuss why Bella changed the way she treated others. Explain that to be happy Bella needed to make friends – and not just be a good dancer.

★ Ask your child what Clare did to warm Bella's heart. How does your child feel when they get a hug from a friend?

★ Emphasize that to have fun and to avoid feeling sad and lonely, your child should be friendly and helpful towards other children. Tell them that it's fun and exciting to meet new people and make new friends, and that they could even try fun activities with their friends, such as dancing.

★ Ask your child to draw a picture of them dancing alone, and another picture of them dancing with their friends. Discuss the different feelings that they may have when they dance alone and when they dance with friends.

Consultant: Cecilia A. Essau
Professor of Developmental
Psychopathology
Director of the Centre for Applied
Research and Assessment in Child and
Adolescent Wellbeing, Roehampton
University, London

Editor: Alexandra Koken
Designer: Andrew Crowson

Copyright © QED Publishing 2012

First published in the UK in 2012 by
QED Publishing
A Quarto Group company
230 City Road
London EC1V 2TT

www.qed-publishing.co.uk

All rights reserved. No part of this publication may be reproduced, stored in a retrieval system, or transmitted in any form or by any means, electronic, mechanical, photocopying, recording, or otherwise, without the prior permission of the publisher, nor be otherwise circulated in any form of binding or cover other than that in which it is published and without a similar condition being imposed on the subsequent purchaser.

A catalogue record for this book is available from the British Library.

ISBN 978 1 84835 899 7

Printed in China